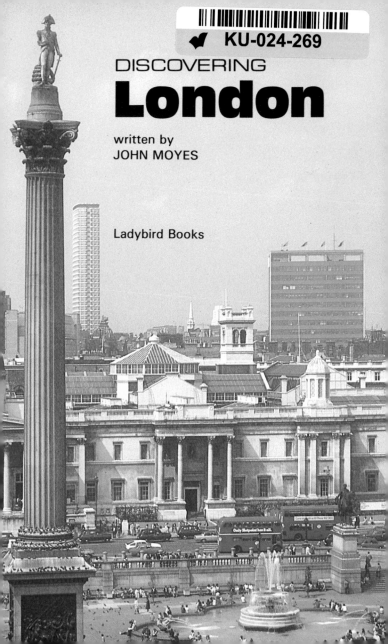

KU-024-269

DISCOVERING
London

written by
JOHN MOYES

Ladybird Books

London is the most daunting city for a stranger and yet, only a little beneath the surface, the most friendly. It is a huge sprawling city, both in size and population. London is the home of Queen Elizabeth II and the Royal Family. It is the seat of the British Government, of Justice and the centre of Finance and Investment.

You must see London on foot, not in a car (you'll never be able to park it!) If you feel tired you can hail a taxi or take one of the red buses for a short journey. The

Pictorial map of LONDON

SCALE		
0	1 KILOMETRES	2

| 0 | ¼ | ½ | ¾ | 1 MILE |

Railways and Stations ▬▬▬
Underground Stations ●

Acknowledgments

The publishers wish to thank Harriet Peacock for her help in compiling this revised edition. Also thanks to J Simpkins of the London Planetarium for the picture on Page 26.

Photographs supplied by: British Tourist Authority – cover, 27, 36/37, 47 (bottom); Roger Bradley – 4/5, 48, 50, 51; Robert Harding Picture Library – 11 (bottom); Jarrold Colour Publications – 14/15; London Regional Transport – back endpaper; John Moyes – title page, 6/7, 8, 9, 14 (top), 16 (bottom), 17, 18, 19, 20, 21, 22, 23, 24, 25, 28/29, 30, 31, 32, 33, 34, 35, 40, 41, 42/43, 44, 45, 47 (top), 48/49, 49; Popperfoto – 10, 11 (top), 12, 13, 16 (top), 21 (top), 38, 39; Syndication International – back cover, 37, 41.

Cover photograph – Big Ben
By courtesy of the British Tourist Authority

British Library Cataloguing in Publication Data
Moyes, John
    Discovering – London.—Rev. ed.
    1. London (England)—Description—1981-
    —Guide-books—Juvenile literature
    I. Title   II. Moyes, John
    Learnabout – London
    914.21′04858   DA679
    ISBN 0-7214-0976-8

Revised edition

Published by Ladybird Books Ltd Loughborough Leicestershire UK
Ladybird Books Inc Lewiston Maine 04240 USA

Waterloo Bridge and the London skyline seen from Hungerford Bridge

Underground system, which is an exciting challenge to the uninitiated, will take you quickly over longer journeys. It is more difficult to travel by public transport during 'rush hours' (between 0800 hours and 0930 hours, and 1700 hours and 1800 hours).

You can stay as long as you like in the places that interest you and not spend so long in those that don't. You can always revisit them another time.

Houses of Parliament

Go first across Westminster Bridge to the South Bank of the River Thames and walk for a while along the river bank. From here you will have the finest view of the Houses of Parliament, or more correctly, the Palace of Westminster. For several hundred years the old Palace was the site of the English Parliament and the home of the king. When King Henry VIII took Whitehall Palace in 1529 and moved to live there, Parliament stayed at Westminster, where it still meets today.

In 1834 it was mostly destroyed by fire and only Westminster Hall, the crypt chapel, the cloisters and the Jewel Tower survived. In 1835 Charles Barry and Augustus Pugin won a national competition to become the architects of a new palace at Westminster. Completed in 1867, their building is said to have as

many windows as there are days in the year.

At the west corner, the Victoria Tower is said to be the largest and tallest square tower in the world. A flag flies from this tower when Parliament is sitting. At the east corner is the famous clock tower, known to everyone as *Big Ben*, though this is really the name of the great bell which chimes the hour.

Walk now towards Big Ben, over Westminster Bridge and, having crossed the river, you will see Queen Boadicea (Boudicca) in her chariot.

At certain times, when Parliament is not sitting, it is possible to visit the Houses of Parliament. You would then see Westminster Hall with its marvellous hammer-beam roof of Sussex oak.

Westminster Abbey

Across Old Palace Yard from the Houses of Parliament
is Westminster Abbey. A church has stood on this site,
once called Thorney Island, since Saxon times. In the
year AD750, a Benedictine Abbey was founded here. It
was known as West Monastery (West-Minster), from its
position two miles west of London's centre. Edward the
Confessor rebuilt it and subsequent kings have restored
it, repaired it and added embellishments of their own.
The most recent addition was the two graceful towers at
its western end. These were designed by Nicholas
Hawksmoor in 1735.

From Norman times English monarchs have been crowned there and, since the thirteenth century, it is there that many have been buried. The Abbey is administered by the Dean and Chapter and technically its status is like that of St George's Chapel at Windsor Castle, known as 'royal peculiar'.

Inside the west door gives the finest view of the Abbey. As you move on inside, past plaques and statues, there is the architectural splendour of Henry VII's Chapel and the Lady Chapel, with its amazingly intricate stonework. By contrast there is the simplicity of the tomb of Edward the Confessor, and also the Coronation Chair. Famous figures from English literature are commemorated in Poets' Corner and some are buried here, like Geoffrey Chaucer and Charles Dickens.

Outside the Abbey, walk through Dean's Yard and into Great Smith Street on the way to Parliament Square.

Westminster Abbey viewed from Dean's Yard

Whitehall

As you cross Parliament Square from the Abbey, notice the statues surrounding it, notably the one of Sir Winston Churchill, who stands facing Parliament.

Walking up Parliament Street, along Whitehall, you pass through the heart of the country's government. Here, until it burned down in 1698, stood Whitehall Palace with its rose-red Tudor brick, its green lawns and shining marble statuary. Now nothing remains of all that self-indulgent splendour but the Banqueting House, designed in Palladian style by Inigo Jones with its beautiful ceiling painted by Rubens. It was from one of the windows of this building that King Charles I stepped to the scaffold in 1649.

Whitehall

The Cenotaph

on Remembrance Day.

A short distance away is Downing Street, where the Prime Minister lives at Number 10.

Further up Whitehall, two of the Queen's Life Guards, on beautifully groomed horses, stand sentry at the entrance of Horse Guards. Try to be there before eleven o'clock (ten o'clock on Sundays) for the Changing of the Guard. This is one of the most colourful events to be seen in everyday London.

Charles I's statue was successfully hidden from Oliver Cromwell's Commonwealth Government by a brazier who had been told to melt it down. It now stands at the top of Whitehall looking down towards the site where King Charles was executed. Behind the statue is a plaque which marks the point in London from which all distances are measured.

In the middle of Whitehall is the Cenotaph where, every year, the Queen lays the first wreath of poppies

One of the Queen's Life Guards

London parks

On through the arch under the Clock Tower is the old
Tilting Yard of Whitehall Palace, now called Horse
Guards Parade. It is here, on the nearest Saturday to her
official birthday in June, that the Queen takes the salute
at the ceremony of Trooping the Colour.

Stretching before you is St James's Park. There are
nearly eight hundred acres of parkland in Central
London. Until 1953 sheep were kept in Hyde Park and
neighbouring Kensington Gardens to crop the grass.

Kensington Gardens

Horse Guards Parade seen from St James's Park

St James's Park is the oldest royal park and lies between the Mall and Birdcage Walk which was redesigned by Charles II, who loved to walk there. The lake is the home of many birds. Ducks and geese waddle pompously along its banks, and you may even see a pelican. Try to go back one evening and stand on the bridge over the lake with floodlit fountains playing on either side, and the London skyline rising above the tree tops.

Buckingham Palace

In the distance, you may hear the sound of a military band. Go along to Buckingham Palace where you may see the Guards as they play themselves out of the forecourt, and march back to barracks. They are a fine sight with their scarlet tunics and the sheen of their bearskins as they march in perfect unison.

Buckingham Palace was purchased by George III for his wife and was rebuilt in 1835 to a design by John Nash. This elegant style, known as Regency, appears frequently in London. 'Buck House', as it has been nicknamed by Londoners, has been the home of the sovereign since Queen Victoria's reign, and the Royal Standard flies overhead whenever Queen Elizabeth is in residence.

Queen Victoria Memorial

In front of the Palace is the Queen Victoria Memorial.

If you turn your back on the Palace and walk under the lime trees which border the Mall, you can turn left into Stable Yard and go to Clarence House and St James's Palace. Clarence House is the home of the Queen Mother, and it was here that, before she ascended the throne, the Queen gave birth to Princess Anne.

Clarence House

St James's Palace

changed: a small but impressive ceremony.

Around the north-west corner of the Palace, Cleveland Row joins Pall Mall and St James's Street. Here, on the southern border of the West End, are the homes of Gentlemen's and Ladies' Clubs. Walk up St James's Street and you will see fine old shops where gentlemen have bought shoes, hats and wine for over two hundred years.

St James's Palace and the West End

St James's Palace became a home for the Royal Family when Whitehall Palace was destroyed in 1698. At the eastern end of the courtyard is the Chapel Royal which has a beautiful painted ceiling attributed to Holbein. Here the choristers still wear a Tudor uniform of scarlet and gold. Shortly after one o'clock you will see the sentries being

Lock and Co. in St James's Street

Continue up St James's Street and turn right into Piccadilly. On the northern side of Piccadilly is Burlington House, home of the Royal Academy of Arts. Ahead of you is Piccadilly Circus itself, the hub of London's West End and the heart of theatreland. The graceful curve of Regent Street is on your left, Shaftesbury Avenue and Leicester Square lie ahead. You should revisit Piccadilly Circus at night when the statue of Eros is given some rest from constant traffic driving round. Now move on down Haymarket to Trafalgar Square.

London Telecom Tower. A modern landmark compared with the old shops in St James's Street

Wine merchants in St James's Street, Berry Bros. and Rudd. Famous for Port and Claret

18

Trafalgar Square

Trafalgar Square was laid out early in the last century to commemorate Admiral Lord Nelson's last victory at the Battle of Trafalgar. Nelson stands heroically on his column overlooking Whitehall, with Admiralty Arch and the Admiralty at his feet. Everything happens here, from protest marches to carol singing round the huge Christmas tree sent to Britain by the people of Norway every year. Nelson is guarded by four stone lions designed by Edwin Landseer.

However, it is not the lions that dominate Trafalgar Square, but the pigeons. If you buy some grain from the vendors to feed them, the pigeons will walk along your arm and even perch on your head.

Admiralty Arch

Behind Nelson is the National Gallery, in which you will find paintings by Rubens, Rembrandt, Constable, Turner and many others. At the north-east corner of the square is the beautiful church of St Martin-in-the-Fields. James Gibbs was the architect, and the vicars of St Martin's have a special tradition of caring for the poor and needy in the true spirit of Christianity.

The National Gallery

In Duncannon Street, by St Martin's, you can find a bus to take you along the Strand. At either end of the crescent of the Aldwych, are two of London's prettiest churches, St Mary-le-Strand, also by James Gibbs, and St Clement Danes by Christopher Wren. It is the latter church you will remember from the children's rhyme "Oranges and Lemons say the bells of St Clement's."

Church of St Mary-le-Strand

21

The Law Courts and the British Museum

At the end of the Strand, the castellated building that faces you, with its romantic turrets and sugar-loaf towers, is the Law Courts, seat of Civil Legislature. This marks the eastern border of London's West End and beyond this lies Fleet Street, the centre of the newspaper world, and the City. Cross the road now and cut through Clement's Inn to Portsmouth Street where you will find a 16th century antique shop that claims to be the original of Charles Dickens' 'Old Curiosity Shop'.

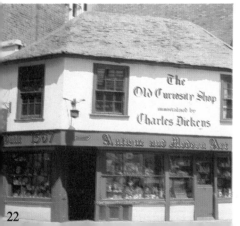

As you walk on into Kingsway, it is a short walk, or a shorter taxi ride, to the British Museum. Nowhere else in the world will you find such a collection of treasures gathered together under the same roof.

The Law Courts

London contains many other museums which you may visit on another day. At South Kensington, easily reached by Underground, are the Victoria and Albert Museum, and the Natural History and Science Museums. In the Science Museum you will find almost every aspect of scientific evolution, from James Watt's original beam engine, to atomic power. Stephenson's *Rocket* is there, as is *Puffing Billy*, and there are many different working models which start at the press of a button.

The British Museum

More museums and exhibitions

The Natural History Museum with its terracotta slabs, tall towers and Romanesque portico is typical of the Victorian architecture found around London. The museum has a fine collection of minerals, meteorites and precious stones as well as examples of every animal, fish, bird and mammal that has ever existed. The huge skeleton of a dinosaur is the collection's pride, as is the life-size model of the Blue Whale.

The Natural History Museum

You should also try to find time to visit the Museum of London in the Barbican near St Paul's. This museum covers over 2000 years of the history of London.

Madame Tussaud's

Next door to Baker Street station is the Waxworks Exhibition of Madame Tussaud's. Here you can rub shoulders with the famous, not only from the pages of history books, but also from the worlds

of politics and art, sport and entertainment. Minute attention has been given to detail, both of the figures themselves and their costume; one mass murderer who appears in the Chamber of Horrors actually sent his suit to Madame Tussaud's the day before his execution. You will be amazed at how small were some of the powerful people of the past! You can also walk through the lower decks of HMS *Victory* during the Battle of Trafalgar and see the gunners as they would have been during the action.

The Planetarium

In the Planetarium you can sit back in your seat while all the stars of the northern hemisphere move across the simulated night sky above you. A superb commentary will recreate for you the superstitious fears and beliefs of your ancestors and speculate on the predictions of astronomers for years to come.

The City

The Lord Mayor's coach passing the Law Courts

The City of London, once a walled fortress, occupies an area of only one square mile. It is full of tradition usually better seen on a Sunday so avoiding the busy weekday traffic. The City is the heart of the Nation's Commerce and the titles of its Guilds or Livery Companies reflect the businesses conducted as early as the 12th century; the Weaver's Company, the Mercers, the Haberdashers, the Goldsmiths, the Fishmongers.

The City is governed by its own Corporation headed by the Lord Mayor. A new Lord Mayor is elected every year, and each November he rides in his elaborate coach, made in 1756, through the streets of the City. After this journey he travels to the Law Courts where he is received by the Queen's representative, the Lord Chief Justice. In the evening, at the Guildhall, he and his Sheriffs give a banquet at which they entertain the Prime Minister and members of the Government.

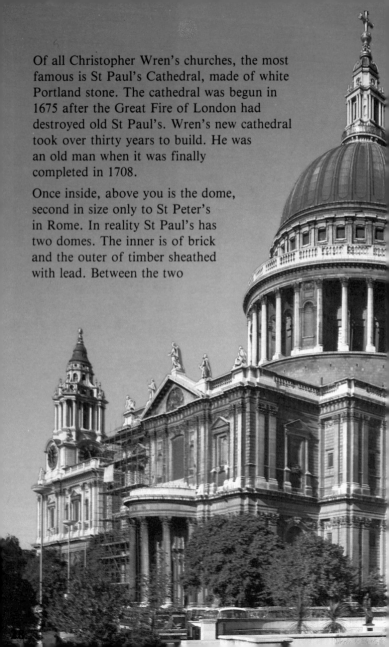

Of all Christopher Wren's churches, the most famous is St Paul's Cathedral, made of white Portland stone. The cathedral was begun in 1675 after the Great Fire of London had destroyed old St Paul's. Wren's new cathedral took over thirty years to build. He was an old man when it was finally completed in 1708.

Once inside, above you is the dome, second in size only to St Peter's in Rome. In reality St Paul's has two domes. The inner is of brick and the outer of timber sheathed with lead. Between the two

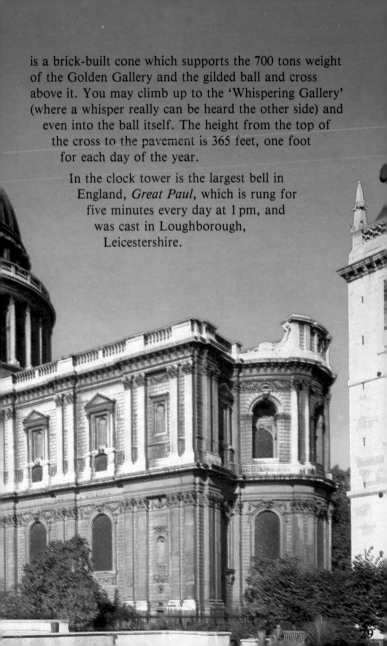

is a brick-built cone which supports the 700 tons weight of the Golden Gallery and the gilded ball and cross above it. You may climb up to the 'Whispering Gallery' (where a whisper really can be heard the other side) and even into the ball itself. The height from the top of the cross to the pavement is 365 feet, one foot for each day of the year.

In the clock tower is the largest bell in England, *Great Paul*, which is rung for five minutes every day at 1 pm, and was cast in Loughborough, Leicestershire.

After a short walk down Prince's Street you are in the City's centre. It is from the steps of the Royal Exchange (picture below) that a new monarch is proclaimed. Ahead and to the left is the Mansion House (picture right) which is the official residence of the Lord Mayor. This contains, among other treasures, a beautiful 8000-piece chandelier of Waterford glass. On your right

is the Bank of England, (picture far right) nicknamed 'Old Lady of Threadneedle Street.'

Down King William Street is the Monument, erected in 1677, to commemorate the Great Fire which broke out in a baker's shop in Pudding Lane. It stands 202 feet from the baker's shop and is 202 feet high. It is possible to climb the 311 steps to the top but the view is now obscured by many high-rise office blocks.

After the Great Fire, Christopher Wren, Royal architect to Charles II, began to rebuild the City. The Monument was partly his, together with three exquisite churches; St Stephen's Walbrook, St Margaret Pattens and St Mary-le-Bow. The last is known all over the world, for a true Cockney must be born within the sound of 'Bow' bells.

Little Venice and the Zoological Gardens

Though you can travel to the zoo by bus or taxi, a more pleasant way is by boat. Near Warwick Avenue underground station, the British Waterways Board have dredged and landscaped the junction of the Grand Union and Regent's Canals to make a pool, overlooked

by pretty houses. This is known as Little Venice. Here you may board a Narrow Boat (it is incorrect to call it a Canal Barge) which will take you along the Regent's Canal to the zoo. It's a fascinating journey and gives a glimpse of the importance of our canal system in the last century.

At the zoo, children may ride a camel, or the very young may be pulled in a cart by a llama. You should also see the sea-

lions being fed. With such
a wide variety of animals
in a lovely setting, the zoo
will give you an afternoon
to remember.

Chessington Zoo

Half-an-hour's ride on a train from Waterloo station will bring you to Chessington Zoo. This is a family zoo, with something for everyone. Apart from the animals, there is a boating lake, a circus, rides and entertainments and a miniature train which will take you right through the grounds.

There is a choice of restaurants and snack bars, and a model village, but of course most important are the animals and the birds, especially the penguins who have their own ornamental lake and the polar bear enclosure, the only one in the world with underwater viewing facilities.

The Thames

Without the river, London would never have been built.
Though diminished now as a port, London can be proud
of the River Thames. Work by the water authorities over
the past twenty years has transformed it from a turgid,
stinking sewer to a home once more for bass, sea-trout,
and even salmon.

You can take the waterbus from Charing Cross pier by
the Embankment underground station, on a delightful
journey to the Tower of London. On the left is
Cleopatra's Needle and across the river is the Royal
Festival Hall. Through Waterloo Bridge, on your right,
you will see the National Theatre and on the left is
Somerset House, for many years the home of the

Registry of Births, Marriages and Deaths (now housed at St Catherine's House, Aldwych). By the Embankment near Somerset House are several permanently moored ships. The *Wellington* is now the Livery Hall of the Honourable Company of Master Mariners, and the *Chrysanthemum* and the *President* are training ships for the Royal Naval Volunteer Reserve. Beyond Blackfriar's Bridge there is another fine view of St Paul's. Sir Christopher Wren lived on the South Bank during the cathedral's construction.

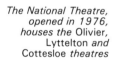

HMS Chrysanthemum *(left) and HMS* President *moored by the Embankment*

The National Theatre, opened in 1976, houses the Olivier, Lyttelton *and* Cottesloe *theatres*

Downriver to the Tower

On down to London Bridge where there stood, until 1749, London's only bridge. Then houses, shops, and even a church stood on the bridge itself. On the South Bank is the beautiful gothic Southwark Cathedral where William Shakespeare used to worship. Passing under the bridge you come to the Pool of London, where HMS *Belfast*, heroine of the Second World War, lies at her moorings. She is now a naval museum.

Tower Bridge, with its two decorated towers, has twin drawbridges, each weighing 1000 tons, both originally operated by hydraulic power. As you disembark at the Tower of London, you should notice Traitor's Gate, now bricked up.

Tower Bridge

The Tower of London

It was William the Conqueror, nine hundred years ago, who first built a fortress here. The White Tower, built of white Caen stone from Normandy in France, is the nucleus of the Tower of London. Later other buildings were added. It has served as a palace as well as a fortress, but it is as a prison that it is known best.

The road of royal succession was a bumpy one, and not always was the throne of England secure and uncontested. Often England was ruled well and justly, but there were times when excessive zeal, greed and stupidity filled the Tower with political prisoners. Three queens were beheaded at the Tower, two princes are supposed to have been murdered, and the screams of the tortured are still said to haunt the dungeons.

The White Tower

You will see the Yeoman Warders in their Tudor uniforms. They are often mis-called 'Beefeaters'. Also in the Tower are the Crown Jewels, heavily guarded. Only once, in Charles II's reign, were they stolen, and the thief got no further than Traitor's Gate. The surprising outcome of his trial was that he was awarded a pension for life, as it was whispered that King Charles himself had instigated the robbery.

St Katherine's Dock

The White Tower, which was whitewashed during Henry III's reign, contains a fine collection of arms and armour and in the Beauchamp Tower you can see the initials and inscriptions on the stone walls carved by the many prisoners who were kept there. The ravens on Tower Green are the last remnants of the royal menagerie of Henry VIII. There is a superstition that should the ravens leave the Tower of London, Britain and the Commonwealth will crumble. Today the ravens' wings are kept severely clipped!

From the Tower you can walk past the cannons and under Tower Bridge to St Katherine's Dock, home of the historic ship collection. This unique collection includes the *Cambria*, a Thames sprit sail barge, the *Nore*, and a lightship vessel. Further down the river, at Woolwich, is the Thames Barrier. Built in 1984, its massive steel gates are designed to prevent the possibility of London ever being flooded.

A hundred years ago the river was full of sailing barges, going to and from the docks with cargoes of imported goods for the little shallow harbours of the Thames estuary.

Thames Sailing Barges at Blackwater, Essex

Downriver to Greenwich

At Tower Pier you can take a launch downtide. A
delightful commentary will tell you of riverside history
and you will see for yourself the wharfs and taverns
where past dark deeds were done. Through Wapping and
Limehouse, Bermondsey and Rotherhithe you will come
to the Isle of Dogs where King Henry VIII is said to
have kept his hunting dogs. At the southern tip of the
Isle is a small park called Island Garden. From here
there is a fine view of Greenwich waterfront on the other
side of the river. As it approaches Greenwich Pier, the
launch will make a wide turn. This will give you the best
view of the Royal Naval College which was built on the

The Royal Naval College, Greenwich

site where Greenwich Palace once stood. Henry VIII was born at Greenwich Palace and so were his daughters, Mary and Elizabeth.

In 1694, Sir Christopher Wren designed the Royal Hospital for Seamen in the Classical style. It was this building which became the Royal Naval College in 1873. The College is open most afternoons and inside you will see Wren's painted hall and chapel. Also note the marvellous ceilings painted in the Baroque style by James Thornhill. Admiral Lord Nelson had his lying in state in the hall before he was buried in St Paul's Cathedral.

Greenwich

At the head of Greenwich Pier is the champion tea
clipper, *Cutty Sark*, which dwarfs the little *Gipsy Moth
IV* in which, in 1966-67, Sir Francis Chichester sailed
single-handed round the world. You can visit both of
these.

Look at the Queen's House, home of the National
Maritime Museum. This was designed by Inigo Jones for
the wife of James I in 1617. The east and west wings of
this elegant white-stone building were not added until
1807. This was the first example of the Palladian style to
appear in England, and is flanked on either side by
magnificent colonnades. The exhibition is set out in

chronological order and starts in the Queen's House in Tudor times when Henry VIII founded the Royal Navy. With models, paintings, relics and actual ships, the museum traces the evolution of ships and seamanship up to the present day.

In Greenwich Park you may climb the hill to Flamsteed House, the original site of the Royal Observatory. Standing on the Zero Meridian of Longitude, you will enjoy one of London's finest views. You could then return from Greenwich by train instead of by launch.

The Queen's House

Hampton Court Palace

The Great Gatehouse

You can travel all the way to Hampton Court Palace by water, but it's a long journey. You would be better to go by train from Waterloo. The Palace has a fascinating history. Like Whitehall Palace, it was built for Cardinal Wolsey, and when he fell from the King's favour, Henry VIII took both palaces for his own. Here he hunted deer and courted some of the ladies who were to become his wives.

During the seventeenth century it became fashionable to build in the style of the Palace of Versailles. Hampton Court was saved from this fate by a shortage of funds.

Instead, King William and Queen Mary settled for renovation, and employed Sir Christopher Wren. In consequence, Hampton Court, set in graceful gardens and bordered by the Thames, embodies some of the very best of British architecture. You can walk through its State Rooms and Royal Apartments which have been beautifully preserved. Here are portraits of Henry VIII

24-hour clock at Hampton Court Palace

and some of his wives and also portraits of the ladies of the Court of Charles II, painted by Sir Peter Lely.

Outside in the orangery, you will see the two hundred year old vine and perhaps lose yourself in the famous Hampton Court maze.

Hampton Court remained the favourite palace of monarchs until, in the middle of the eighteenth century, George III is said to have taken a dislike to the State Apartments preferring instead the quietness of Kew.

The maze at Hampton Court, laid out by William III's royal gardeners in the 1690s

By river to Kew Gardens

From just outside
Hampton Court Palace it's
a leisurely journey by
launch down to Kew.
Through Teddington Lock
you will be in the tideway,
soon through Ham and
Richmond, and in Kew.
From here it is a short
walk to Kew Gardens.

The Royal Botanical
Gardens are the home of
serious scientific research.
Plants of all kinds are

grown there, and from studies of them, botanists have been able to recommend, for example, what kind of wheat should be grown in Canada, and what plant will yield the most rubber in Malaysia. But this is not just a research station. In Kew you will find flower beds and parkland and perhaps have a picnic by the Pagoda. The Plant House is like a hot, South American jungle.

London at night

In London in the evening there is the finest selection of entertainment to be found anywhere in the world. There is Opera and Ballet (for which you must book well in advance) and at the Theatre, your choice is unlimited. A spectacular musical is only across the road from a Shakespeare season or a knock-about farce. You may see, in the flesh, the actors who, through film and television, have become household names.

There are lots of discos, jazz and concerts, particularly the summer season of Promenade Concerts (known as the 'Proms') at the Royal Albert Hall. Over the river, at the Royal Festival Hall you will find the widest possible range of programmes, international orchestras, conductors and soloists. Acoustically, this is one of the finest concert halls in the world.

After the concert, stand where you began your tour of London in this book, on the banks of the Thames, and see the lights of the Victoria Embankment reflected in the river. Cross to Waterloo Bridge and you will see St Paul's, flood-lit.

Whenever you visit London, whether your stay is a long one or even if you only have a short time, everyone is assured of something to wonder at, something which will entertain and every visitor will take away many happy memories of this fascinating city.

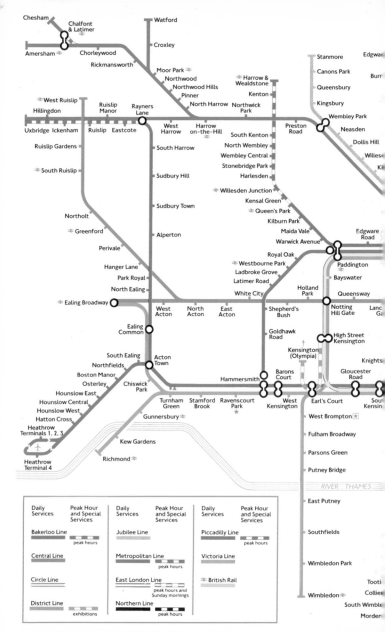

Chesham
Chalfont & Latimer
Amersham
Chorleywood
Rickmansworth
Watford
Croxley
Moor Park
Northwood
Northwood Hills
Pinner
North Harrow
West Ruislip
Hillingdon
Ruislip Manor
Rayners Lane
West Harrow
Harrow on-the-Hill
Harrow & Wealdstone
Kenton
Northwick Park
Stanmore
Canons Park
Queensbury
Kingsbury
Wembley Park
Edgwa
Burr
Neasden
Dollis Hill
Willese
Uxbridge
Ickenham
Ruislip
Eastcote
Ruislip Gardens
South Ruislip
South Harrow
Sudbury Hill
Sudbury Town
Alperton
South Kenton
North Wembley
Wembley Central
Stonebridge Park
Harlesden
Preston Road
Ki
Northolt
Greenford
Perivale
Hanger Lane
Park Royal
North Ealing
Willesden Junction
Kensal Green
Queen's Park
Kilburn Park
Maida Vale
Warwick Avenue
Royal Oak
Westbourne Park
Ladbroke Grove
Latimer Road
White City
Edgware Road
Paddington
Bayswater
Queensway
Ealing Broadway
West Acton
North Acton
East Acton
Shepherd's Bush
Goldhawk Road
Holland Park
Notting Hill Gate
Lanc
Ga
Ealing Common
Acton Town
Kensington (Olympia)
High Street Kensington
Knights
South Ealing
Northfields
Boston Manor
Osterley
Hounslow East
Hounslow Central
Hounslow West
Hatton Cross
Heathrow Terminals 1, 2, 3
Chiswick Park
Turnham Green
Stamford Brook
Ravenscourt Park
Hammersmith
Barons Court
West Kensington
Earl's Court
Gloucester Road
Sou
Kensin
Gunnersbury
Kew Gardens
Richmond
West Brompton
Fulham Broadway
Parsons Green
Putney Bridge
Heathrow Terminal 4
RIVER THAMES
East Putney
Southfields
Wimbledon Park
Wimbledon
Tooti
Collie
South Wimble
Morden

This
Treasure Cove Story
belongs to

THE SWORD IN THE STONE

A CENTUM BOOK 978-1-912396-40-5
Published in Great Britain by Centum Books Ltd.
This edition published 2018. 1 3 5 7 9 10 8 6 4 2

Centum Books Ltd, 20 Devon Square, Newton Abbot,
Devon, TQ12 2HR, UK.

www.centumbooksltd.co.uk | books@centumbooksltd.co.uk
CENTUM BOOKS Limited Reg.No. 07641486.

A CIP catalogue record for this book is available
from the British Library.

Printed in China.

centum

A Treasure Cove Story

WALT DISNEY'S
The Sword in the Stone

Adapted by Carl Memling

Based on the Walt Disney motion picture
The Sword in the Stone, suggested
by an original story *The Sword in the Stone*
by T H White

Wart was a lonely page living in the great stone castle of Sir Ector. Nobody called Wart by his proper name, which was Arthur. Everybody called him just Wart.

Sir Ector had a big, lazy son named Kay, who liked to stretch out in the sun and doze. His favourite spot was a grassy bank near the drawbridge.

But poor Wart had to work and work.
He scrubbed pans and scoured pots in the castle cookhouse.

He helped the castle carpenter.

He polished armour
for the armourer.

He swept the castle stables clean.

Poor Wart. He was all tired out.

But one day, there was a clap of thunder
in the great hall of the castle.

There was a puff of smoke and there stood
a strange old man.

'My name is Merlin. I am a wizard,' he said.
'Wart needs lessons. So I have come.'

Sir Ector and Kay laughed and hooted.

'Lessons! What does Wart need lessons for?
Go away, old man,' said Sir Ector.

Merlin waved his wand. And right there inside
the great hall it began to snow! It snowed and
it snowed and it snowed.

Well, Sir Ector changed his mind. He let Merlin
stay on and said, 'Give Wart lessons, if you like.'

Nobody understood why Wart needed lessons,
but Merlin began to give him lessons.
He led Wart down to the moat one day.
And he waved his wand.

Wart began to shrink. He shrank smaller and smaller.
Suddenly, he changed into a little fish and fell into
the water.

At first it was great fun.

But then a big fish came along.

The big fish wanted to catch the little
fish for lunch.

Poor little Wart. What could he do?

He used his head.

He hid in a clump of seaweed so the big fish couldn't find him.

'Very good,' said Merlin. 'You learned your lesson, Wart. *When in trouble, use your head.*'

Merlin kept on with
the lessons. Once, he changed
Wart into a squirrel.

As a squirrel, Wart stored nuts
in trees. He learned to be ready for
what tomorrow might bring.

Another time, Merlin changed him into a bird.

As a bird, Wart flew high in the sky. And seeing the world from way up there, he learned many things.

Wart grew wiser and wiser.

But still nobody understood. Why did Wart need lessons?

One wintry day, a knight came to the castle.
He brought news of a great tournament to be
held in London. The winner would be crowned
king of all England!

'A tournament's the very thing we need to choose
an English king,' said Sir Ector. He thought that Kay
would win.

And so they all rode off.

Kay sat on a prancing horse. His armour glistened in the sunlight.

But Wart was just a lowly squire. He rode a plodding donkey all the way to London town.

After many days and nights, they came at last to
the tournament field. There was a blast of trumpets.
And the tilting started.

Kay smiled proudly. Soon, with spear and sword,
he would fight to win the crown.

Suddenly, Wart ran from the field. He had
forgotten Kay's sword! It was back at the inn
where they had slept.

Wart ran as fast as he could. But when
he got to the inn, it was closed.

Poor Wart – where could he find a sword?
He ran and ran. In a churchyard, he saw a marble
stone. On it stood a steel anvil. And stuck through
the anvil was a gleaming sword.

A sword!

Wart quickly pulled it out and carried
it back to the tournament field.

'But that's not Kay's sword!' cried Sir Ector
when he saw it.

Then he saw some letters written in gold
on the sword.

This is what the letters said:

WHO SO PULLETH OUT THIS SWORD
OF THIS STONE AND ANVIL IS RIGHTWISE
KING BORN OF ALL ENGLAND.

Sir Ector read that. And so did all the other
noblemen. Now they knew. The tournament *wasn't*
the thing whereby to choose a king. *The sword was!*

But how could Wart have pulled it out? There
must be some mistake.

They all went to the churchyard. Wart put back the
sword into the stone.

Everyone tried, but the sword wouldn't move. Only
Wart could pull it out again. So it was no mistake.

But kings must be wise. Kings must know many
things. How could Wart be a king?

Wart was wise enough. And he knew enough. For that's what the lessons had been for – to prepare Wart to be king.

And Wart became a great king, known forever after as King Arthur.

Treasure Cove Stories

Book list may be subject to change.

An ongoing series to collect and enjoy!